Tommy
the Theatre Cat

Maureen Potter

Illustrated by David Rooney

THE O'BRIEN PRESS
DUBLIN

This edition first published 2005
by The O'Brien Press Ltd.,
20 Victoria Road, Dublin 6, Ireland.
Tel: +353 1 4923333; Fax: +353 1 4922777
E-mail: books@obrien.ie
Website: www.obrien.ie
Originally published 1986 by The O'Brien Press Ltd.

ISBN: 0-86278-919-2

British Library Cataloguing-in-Publication Data
Potter, Maureen
Tommy the theatre cat
1.Cats - Juvenile fiction 2.Theatre - Juvenile fiction
3.Children's stories
I.Title II.Rooney, David, 1962-
823.9'14[J]

the arts
council
schomhairle
ealaíon

The O'Brien Press receives assistance from
Editing; typesetting; layout; design: The O'Brien Press Ltd
Printing: Cox & Wyman Ltd

Contents

Chapter One

Tommy the Cat

TOMMY WAS A MOST UNUSUAL CAT. Not that he was a rare breed or a very strange colour. He had a rich, dark coat, four white paws and a puzzled expression on his white face, as if he was forever asking a question. Perhaps he was – cats are very curious creatures. Tommy was unusual because he was a theatre cat. He lived in a big theatre in the centre of the city, and his job was to keep the place free of rats and mice.

The theatre was a big rambling place with rows and rows of red seats stretching right up to the roof. On either side were boxes with red chairs that Tommy found warm and cosy when cold winds blew through the draughty old place. One chair in particular was soft and roomy, and this was Tommy's favourite. He wasn't to know that he shared it with the President of the country! Not at the same time, of course.

The lady who cleaned the boxes tried in vain to keep Tommy from his favourite seat, but no matter how firmly she locked the door he still got in. She didn't know how he managed it – but she had never seen Tommy do his death-defying leap from the adjoining box! Tommy could not understand why the cleaning lady wanted to keep him out of his favourite box, but then there were many things about his big home that Tommy did not understand.

For a few hours at night it was ablaze with lights and full of noisy people, then suddenly it was quiet and dark except for the creak of some old board settling back into place after all those feet. Then sometimes, on cold afternoons, the theatre would be full of chattering children who would scream and shout at the people on the stage.

On those days Tommy would retire to the comfort of the theatre wardrobe. The ladies there let him stretch out beside the radiator until the silence outside told him that the 'screamers' had departed. Then he would pick his way between the seats, through a carpet of ice-cream tubs and sweet-papers, wondering about this

strange tribe that invaded his home from time to time.

They always came on cold, wet days. Perhaps they were seeking warmth and comfort, like the mice who occasionally trespassed on his territory. But they certainly were not as quiet as the mice. The only good thing he could say about them was that they often left ice-cream tubs that were not completely empty, and Tommy was fond of ice cream. The old lady who worked in the little cloakroom at the back of the theatre often shared an ice cream with him. But, strangely enough, on the days the children came she seemed too fussed and busy to bother with him.

And, of course, the cleaning lady, the guardian of the boxes, she was the most annoyed of all on those days. So angry and taken up with other things that she would forget to lock his favourite box and he could sneak in and settle down in that big red chair.

And it was while he was snoozing peacefully on the President's chair one day that Tommy first encountered the cat who had a man inside!

Chapter 2

The Man in
the Cat

TOMMY WAS DOZING in his big red chair. The theatre was empty, but on the stage he could hear people talking and, in the background, the sound of hammering. That meant they were preparing for a show, and as the days were getting colder very soon the screamers would be back.

Suddenly he heard a voice calling, 'Tommy, Tommy, come along, please.'

I must be dreaming, he thought.

Usually at this time the cry was, 'Get that cat out of here.'

Then the voice again, 'Tommy, Tommy. Cat on stage, please.'

Tommy peeped over the edge of the box, and to his amazement the biggest cat he had ever seen bounded onto the stage. Tommy had never known his brothers and sisters, but often at night he looked out the windows and saw other cats passing silently across the waste ground opposite the theatre. They seemed to be the same size as himself, but this cat on the stage was the biggest he had ever seen. And it was walking on its hind legs! He almost toppled out of the box in surprise.

The monster was being introduced to someone Tommy recognised – the small lady with glasses who often moved into the room beside the stage, with the name 'Maureen Potter' on the door. A friendly lady who always had a pat for him and let him settle down on her couch as long as he did not lie on her clothes. Once, in a kittenish mood, he had played with some ribbons and knocked down a head of hair, and the small lady got very cross indeed. But she was usually a very friendly person.

And she must be a very brave one too, for there she was holding the paw of this huge cat. Then, music started up and the pair began to dance. Tommy looked on, eyes like saucers, feeling very small indeed. If this creature could do all these things, Tommy would soon be out of a job. What mouse or rat would venture in while a cat that size was at large? And to think it had taken his name too!

Everyone finally moved off stage, and

Tommy ventured out of his hiding place to get a closer look at the intruder. He saw the big cat go into a dressing room, so he settled down on the landing above to watch. Shortly afterwards the door opened and Tommy crouched down nervously, but only a small man with glasses emerged. The man left the door open behind him, and after a while Tommy padded quietly downstairs and peeped into the room. There was no sign of the monster. Tommy crept cautiously inside. Then he almost died of shock, almost lost several of his nine lives. The monster was hiding behind the door! Tommy was trapped.

He dashed under a table and prepared to defend himself. But no attack came, and eventually, nervously, he peeped out. The monster was still behind the door, but he looked flat and very still. Perhaps he was asleep? Perhaps Tommy could slide past him to safety?

Tommy was just at the door when he heard footsteps. It was the man returning. Tommy darted back under the table. Then, in the big mirror on the wall, he saw the man take off his shoes, put his glasses on the table, and then ... and then ... he climbed into the cat! The giant gazed at himself in the mirror, then left the room. Tommy was horrified. There was a man in that huge cat! Was there a man in every cat? Was there a small man inside him waiting to get out? He opened his mouth very wide and stared into the mirror. He could not see any man down there, only his red tongue and shining teeth. How did the man get past those

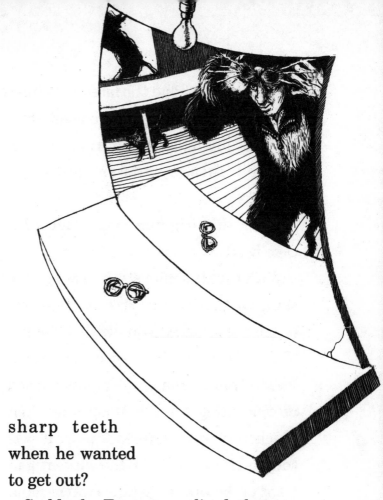

sharp teeth
when he wanted
to get out?

Suddenly Tommy realised that
there was someone looking at him from
the doorway. It was the big cat, but this
time it had the man's face – a smiling
face.

'Hello, puss,' said the face, 'you must be Tommy. I'm delighted to meet you.' He put out a big paw and Tommy backed into a corner, snarling nervously.

'Does this frighten you? Here, I'll take it off.'

With that the man stepped out of the skin, for that is what it was. He laid it on the floor and said, with a laugh, 'C'mon, Tommy, have a good look at it.'

After much thought, Tommy sniffed at the thing on the floor and then touched it with an uneasy paw. It was soft and furry, just like the white rug in front of the fire in that nice warm room upstairs. He had got in there once but a large man with a pipe had chased him away, shouting loudly to his old foe, the cleaning lady, 'Get that cat out of here.' Tommy walked across the skin, and, now much braver, began to shake and worry that big face and whiskers that had worried him so much before.

'Hold on, Tommy,' said the man, with a grin, 'That's my living you're attacking. Here, have a piece of chicken.'

He picked out a piece of chicken from his sandwich and put it on the floor. Tommy moved to take it and the man stroked his back.

'What a lovely coat you have,' he said. 'I wish I had it.'

Tommy backed away from the food. Was this a trick to get his skin? The man laughed.

'Eat your food. I'm not after your fur. We cats must stick together.'

Just then a voice below called, 'Tommy, Tommy,' and the man, picking up the cat skin said, 'C'mon partner, let's give them a double act.' Tommy followed him cautiously downstairs and when they walked on stage together everyone laughed.

'I see you have an understudy, Terry,' said the small lady with the glasses, picking up Tommy and giving him a hug. So, the cat man was called Terry.

But a tall man in a sweater interrupted the fun.

'Right, Terry,' he said, 'Dick Whittington has put his bundle up in this tree. See if you can reach it.'

The cat man got down on all fours, stretched up a paw, but could not reach the bundle. I could reach that, thought Tommy, and with a quick spring he shot up the tree and knocked down the bundle. Unfortunately, the stage tree was not made for climbing and with a

loud clatter the tree and Tommy both came crashing onto the stage. Everyone laughed again, except the stage hand who had to sort out the mess and the director who wanted to get on with the rehearsal. So Tommy was put in the wings to watch his new-found friend go through his paces. And every now and again Terry came over, patted him and asked, 'How am I doing, partner?'

Tommy and Terry became close friends and every night Tommy waited at the stage door for his cat man to arrive. He would follow him up to the dressing room and sit beside the mirror while Terry prepared for the show. Then he'd settle at the side of the stage and watch critically while Dick Whittington and his Cat went through all their adventures. Tommy purred with delight when Dick was made Lord Mayor of London and told all the audience that he could not have succeeded without his faithful Cat.

One night, as Tommy waited at the stage door for his friend, he noticed sadly that lots of flowers were being delivered to the theatre. He knew from experience that this meant the show was coming to an end. For some reason he could never understand, the stage people gave one another flowers on the last night, and the following day they were all gone. So he watched with a heavy heart as Dick Whittington and his Cat went through the story he now knew so well.

When the curtain was down and the show was finally over, Tommy went to visit his friend and found him packing away his cat suit in a basket. The room looked cold and lonely without the clothes and the bottles and brushes that had become so familiar. Terry, reading Tommy's thoughts, said, 'I wonder who will be in here next week?' Then he picked Tommy up, gave him a pat, and said, 'Come along, I have something to show you.'

He carried him across the stage, and there, in a quiet corner, was a little wooden house with the name TOMMY painted across it. The doorway was a flap that could be pushed open and on it was a star.

'It's your own dressing room,' said Terry. 'Go in and have a look.'

Tommy pushed open the flap and inside was a carpet made of the same material as the cat suit that had frightened him so much before. He sniffed all round the cosy interior and

when he came out his friend had gone.

Tommy watches every year when the winter comes to see if the pantomime will have a cat in it. His friend has not returned since, but every Christmas a card arrives with a simple message, 'Happy Christmas, Tommy, see you again someday.' Fred, the stage doorman, pins the cards up on the wall of Tommy's 'dressing room'. The cards come from theatres all over the world, but Tommy is hoping that one Christmas it won't be a card that arrives but instead his old friend the Man in the Cat.

Chapter 3

Cat at Work!

TOMMY WAS DISAPPOINTED.
Another pantomime in rehearsal but
sadly no sign of Terry, the Man in the
Cat. The small lady with the glasses
was back again, marching around the
stage blowing a pipe, followed by lots of
children. The children always made a
fuss of Tommy and often brought him
titbits which they left outside the little
box now known by all as Tommy's
Room. His one-time adversary, the
cleaning lady, was delighted with his

new home as it meant he no longer tried to outwit her to get into the President's box. She even took out his cat-skin carpet from time to time and gave it a good going over with her vacuum cleaner. The first time she did

this Tommy thought she was stealing
his prized possession and he howled
loudly for help. When she returned his
carpet fresh and clean, he felt rather
sheepish. It didn't pay to jump to
sudden conclusions, as he was to

discover again the very next day.

Tommy had snuggled down in his box after quite a hearty breakfast provided by Mac, his favourite stage hand. The children were rehearsing on stage.

Suddenly he heard them screaming, 'RATS, RATS, RATS!' Tommy dashed to the stage and there on the backcloth were hundreds of rats. Big brown rats, snarling and baring their teeth.

Tommy leapt into action. He climbed up the cloth and hit out left and right at his foes. It was very difficult, hanging on grimly with one paw while flailing away with the other. In spite of all his efforts he did not seem to be making contact with the enemy.

Suddenly the cloth went all white and the rats disappeared! Digging his paws into the cloth, Tommy looked

down. The director
seemed in a terrible rage.
The children were
rolling around,
shrieking with
laughter. Mac,
the stage hand who
had provided his
breakfast, was
shaking his fist at
Tommy. Then with an
awful r-r-ripping sound the cloth
split apart and Tommy came
crashing down. He did not wait
for the now familiar cry, 'Get
that cat out of here', but stalked
away to his Room with as much
dignity as he could muster.

He would never understand
these people. First they shouted for
help. Then when he tried to do his job

some of them got very angry and the rest just laughed at him. Of course, Tommy didn't know the rats were on film and he had just wrecked the opening scene of the Pied Piper. What he did know was that the next time they called for help he wouldn't be so quick to come to the rescue. And that time was not too far away.

It was another confusing day. Tommy had heard the bells ringing in the nearby church. That usually meant that the theatre would be closed and he could have a nice restful day. He could rove all over the place, even as far as that room with the white rug and the fire. However, today the stage was a hive of activity. Rows of chairs were being set out with a little stand in front of each one. Strange people with cases of all shapes and sizes were milling around, with a small, fussy man shouting at them, 'Get settled please. The maestro will be here soon.'

The newcomers were fussy too – 'It's very cold up here', they said, or 'Not at all, it's too stuffy', or 'We must have more light, it's too dark up here.'

Then there was a flurry of excitement at the stage door as a small grey-haired man, with a short pointed beard, arrived. He bustled onto the stage, wearing a long black coat and furry hat. He handed his coat and hat to the fussy man and got up on a little platform in front of the orchestra. He waved a short stick at the musicians and as if by magic they began to play.

But after a short while he shouted, 'No, no,' banging his stick angrily, and the music stopped. He spoke sharply to the players who looked very worried.

Tommy could not understand this. The man with the beard only had a small stick yet there was a man at the back who had two sticks with knobs on them. Surely the man with the two sticks would win if it came to a fight? He watched eagerly to see if they would come to blows, but even 'Two Sticks' seemed to be afraid of the bearded one. Soon the orchestra began to play a soft dreamy tune and Tommy decided to have a nap. He was just about to settle down when a passing stage hand stepped on his tail. Tommy gave a howl of pain that echoed all round the stage. Some of the musicians tittered and looked nervously at the Maestro. He stared down at them and then asked, with a twinkle in his eye, 'Who played that note?' Everybody laughed, and Mac took the opportunity to pick

Tommy up and hurry with him to the wardrobe. There the wounded one sat beside the radiator and began to nurse his throbbing tail.

Tommy's tail was feeling better. One of his wardrobe ladies had treated him to a saucer of milk. He could hear the music in the background, but suddenly it was interrupted by screaming and shouting.

The stage manager dashed

into the room.

'Come on, Tommy,' he shouted, 'there's a mouse on stage.'

Tommy cocked one eye, but did not move. He wasn't going to rush into another situation like the children and the disappearing rats. The stage manager picked him up bodily and carried him onto the stage. What a sight! All the ladies were standing on their chairs, screaming. The Maestro was sitting on his platform, his head in his hands. The man with the two sticks was down on the stage floor hammering at cases and bags while some of the men cheered him on. Tommy dutifully searched the stage, but there was no mouse to be seen.

Eventually, calm was restored. The fussy man assured all the ladies that the mouse had gone. The bearded one got down off his platform. One of the men picked up a big brass instrument and gave it a blow. Out shot the mouse from his hiding place and landed right in the midst of the ladies! A flying mouse! In a flash the ladies jumped up on their chairs again, screaming even louder than before.

The terrified mouse scuttled from drum to drum pursued by the hammering drummer.

The noise was deafening. The mouse dashed through the stage door, with

Tommy in close pursuit, but made his escape through a small hole in a wall nearby. Tommy stood guard for some time, then returned to the theatre. The man with the beard was coming out, shaking his head.

'I'm going to lunch, puss,' he said. 'I hope you have just had yours?'

He nodded happily when Tommy licked his lips. It wasn't really a fib, just someone else jumping to a wrong conclusion. Anyway, that mouse would never return to face all those screaming

ladies. What a morning it had been!
And usually those church bells meant it
was to be a day of rest.

Chapter 4

Tommy on Stage

TOMMY HAD BEEN a long time looking at plays and players from the wings, but he never dreamt that one day he would appear on stage himself. It all happened when a strange man called Spike, with long grey hair, came to perform at the theatre. He was a friendly man and made a fuss of Tommy the first time they met on the stairs. Tommy watched to see what the man did on stage. Did he wear a cat skin like the man in the pantomime? Had

he a band like the man
with the beard? To his
surprise, this man
just sat on a couch
and spoke to the
people. It was a
v   e   r   y
comfortable
looking couch
and Tommy
decided he
would try it out
when everyone
had gone home.

Tommy was not
paying much attention to the man on
stage, but vaguely heard him say
something about a cat laughing.
Suddenly, the man walked into the
wings, picked Tommy up and carried
him onto the stage. Tommy blinked at

the bright lights, opened his mouth to protest, but the man said quickly, 'I told you it would make a cat laugh.'

There was a big laugh from the people out there in the darkness and they all clapped loudly. The man gave Tommy a friendly pat and set him down gently on the couch. It was as soft and comfortable as it looked, but Tommy still felt uneasy. He had no business being out there even though it was all that man's fault. He was about to run off to the safety of his box when he saw the stage hands grinning at him from the side of the stage. They weren't shaking their fists like they had done when he attacked all those rats, so it must be alright to stay. Besides, the man was stroking him with a firm hand and seemed quite happy to share the couch and the limelight. So Tommy curled himself up in a ball and that made the people laugh and clap again. Tommy could see nothing funny in a cat settling himself comfortably, but if it kept them happy he would do it again. He did so, and they laughed and clapped again. But the lights were warm, the couch was soft, and after a few more turns Tommy settled down for a little nap.

He was startled from his doze by a terrible, piercing noise. The man had picked up a trumpet and blown it right behind his ear. Tommy got an awful fright but the man said, 'Nobody sleeps when I'm working,' and all the people laughed and clapped again. Tommy didn't think it a bit funny and when he saw the man putting the trumpet to his lips again he took off. Even though the man was now playing a pretty tune

Tommy continued his journey. The man made everyone laugh again by shouting after him, 'Come back, Tommy, I don't play that badly.'

Tommy wasn't sure whether the man was cross with him or not so he stayed in his Room until the show was over. Then he heard footsteps approaching and his name being called. I'll pretend I'm deaf, he said to himself. Deafened by that trumpet. Then, in spite of his deafness, he heard something being poured into his dish, and the voice saying, 'Come on, Tommy, have some cream.' He put his head out and there was the trumpet man with a large carton of cream. Tommy came out, rubbing his ear.

The man laughed. 'Sorry about the trumpet, puss. I'll be more careful. You were a great help. See you tomorrow.'

The next night Tommy sat at the side of the stage wondering what he should do. His mind was made up for him by his friend Mac, who pushed him onto the stage. All the people laughed when they saw him, so Tommy jumped up on the couch and sat down. The trumpet man let on to be very surprised by Tommy's arrival and asked, 'Hello, what do you want?'

This confused Tommy, but he tried his curling up trick, and everyone laughed and clapped. So the man said, 'That's right, make yourself at home', and went on talking to the people. Tommy pretended to be asleep, but had one eye half open to see if that terrible trumpet was going to be used again. The man picked it up and said quietly to the people, 'He loves this,' but before he could blow it Tommy had disappeared from the stage. Everybody laughed, so Tommy felt he had done the right thing. And so he had, for after the show he got another bowl of cream. This is easy work, he thought.

The next night went well also, but the following night was a disaster. A 'cat'-astrophe, in fact! The show was on. Tommy was trotting past the Green Room on his way to the side of the stage when Annie called him. She was an old friend who worked in the Green Room. This is the room where the actors relax over a cup of tea or a drink when not on stage. Annie often brought Tommy a little treat and this night she had brought him some lovely fish. He could get the tempting smell as she unwrapped it, and he licked his lips as she spread it on a big blue plate.

Everything else was forgotten, and Tommy tucked in to a tasty meal. When he had licked up the last scrap he settled down to wash his face. In the distance he thought he heard that awful cry, 'Get that cat out of here.' He must be mistaken. Annie had invited him in and there was no one else around. Then he realised what they were saying: 'Get that cat out here. He should be on stage.' Tommy dashed out. Spike was playing his trumpet. Tommy was just about to go on when Mac stopped him. He looked very cross.

'You're late,' he said, 'you were off.'

That's what theatre people say if someone is missing when they should be on stage. Tommy felt very ashamed of himself. He decided not to

49

go back to his box but to rejoin Annie in the Green Room. He hid himself under the counter out of harm's way. When the show had finished he heard the trumpet man coming into the Green Room.

'Where's that rapscallion of a cat?' he shouted. 'He let me down tonight.'

'It was my fault,' explained Annie. 'I delayed him.'

'Ah,' said the man, 'cats are not dependable. Next week I'll get a dog.'

But Annie had the last word. 'Well, if you do,' she said, 'make sure his name is in the programme. Our Tommy is not mentioned at all this week.'

The man went off, laughing, but when Tommy returned to his box there was no cream in his dish. At least the fish had been delicious.

Tommy stayed near at hand next night in case he was needed, but he was not called on stage. He was disappointed, as the man had not seemed too cross the night before and, besides, Annie had explained. Still, you never knew with these stage people. They were a strange lot. He was just about to return to his box when the trumpet man called him. He picked Tommy up and carried him to the front of the stage.

'This is my mate, Tommy,' he told the audience. 'He has been a great help to me this week.'

There was great applause and Tommy felt very important indeed. After the show he found his dish full of cream and beside his box were six tins of his favourite food. So, he was back in favour!

The sound of the church bells next day told Tommy there would be no show, unless the orchestra arrived to disturb that mouse again. But the only visitor was Mac, who called in to open a tin of food for Tommy's dinner. Tommy spent the afternoon on the couch and even practised a few of his settling down turns which seemed to please people so much. The following morning, as he went past the trumpet man's dressing room, he heard some very strange noises inside. Gingerly, he pushed the door open and saw, to his horror, that the place was full of dogs. Big dogs, small dogs, black dogs, white dogs – all barking furiously as Tommy's head appeared round the door.

So, the trumpet man was not joking, thought Tommy. He got all these dogs

to replace me. How will they all fit on the couch?

Just then a small fat lady came rushing up the stairs.

'It's a cat!' she shrieked. 'A cat. He's upsetting my darlings. Shoo. Shoo.'

Here we go again, thought Tommy – 'Get that cat out of here.' And so it turned out. His box was moved into a small room well away from the stage and the door was closed whenever the dogs were on the scene. Tommy soon realised that this was a new show and that Madame Fifi and her Cute Canines were part of it. He could hear

them barking as they
came downstairs and,
even worse, he could hear
the people applauding a lot
when they finished their act.

One night he slipped out of the
room before the door was closed
and climbed up to join Willy, the fly
man, on his narrow platform far above
the stage. Willy was the man who

55

raised and lowered the curtains and scenery, and, looking down, Tommy could see the dogs doing their tricks. They jumped through hoops and rode on little bikes. The people seemed to like them very much. At the end of each trick the fat lady took something from a table just off stage and fed it to the dogs. Tommy wondered about this food. Did it have some magic that made them perform so well? They seemed very strong too, because for their last trick two dogs stood on the backs of the three biggest dogs and the small white dog climbed right to the top of the pile. Once up there he reared up on his hind legs and got great applause. Tommy felt very jealous indeed.

Next night while the dogs were performing Tommy slipped out quietly to get a look at their food. He waited until they were doing their last trick and as the small dog climbed up to his place Tommy jumped onto the table. The big black dog at the bottom of the pile spotted him, barked furiously and made a dash towards the table to protect the food. All the other dogs wobbled around and then came tumbling down, with the little white dog on top of the lot. The fat lady screamed at them and, in the confusion, Tommy dashed back to his box. He could hear lots of barking and yelping and shouting outside. After some time he heard the door being opened and Mac saying to the fat lady, 'I'm telling you it was not the cat. He's locked in here.' The light was switched on and Tommy came out of his box yawning innocently and blinking at the light.

'There he is, Missus,' said Mac. 'It was your dogs' fault.'

As he closed the door Mac winked at Tommy and wagged a finger. Did he know the truth or was he just guessing?

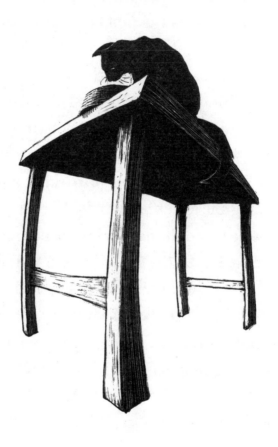

Chapter 5

The Theatre Closes

THE SCREAMERS WERE BACK. From the safety of the wardrobe Tommy could hear them shouting at Aladdin and his friends. He hoped they were too busy screaming to finish all their ice creams. He looked forward to finding some half-empty tubs under the seats when they left.

He wasn't enjoying this pantomime much. It was full of bangs and flashes, and one day during rehearsals he got his whiskers badly singed. All his old friends were back except the man in the cat, but they did not seem very happy. There was a strange feeling about the place. He could not figure it out, but there was something unusual going on. When he went into the wardrobe one of the ladies said sadly, 'Poor Tommy, what's going to happen to you at all, at all?' And the other had said, 'What's going to happen to all of

us?' There was a strange man in the wardrobe, too, counting everything and writing things down in a book. He was not a friend of the wardrobe ladies because when they made their tea they never offered him a cup.

When the screamers had gone Tommy hurried downstairs to see what ice creams they had left. As he passed the dressing room nearest the stage the small lady with the glasses picked him up and gave him a hug. Soon they were surrounded by men with cameras, and the flashes made Tommy blink. They affected the lady too, for when he looked up she had tears in her eyes. She gave Tommy tea in her room, but they were interrupted from time to time by people coming in to talk. Many of the visitors were in tears and Tommy felt that those photographers who made

people blink and cry should not be allowed in at all.

As the show finished that night Tommy was amazed to see lots of flowers being carried onto the stage. That meant it was the last night – but why was it ending so soon? The screamers had not been in that often and Tommy always used their visits as a guide. When the curtain came down the audience clapped and cheered. He had never heard such applause yet no one on stage seemed happy. They were all in tears, and the more they cried the more the people clapped, which seemed very cruel indeed. As they came off stage many of them picked Tommy up and gave him a hug. After a while his coat was damp with tears, and he decided to retreat to his box to ponder on this very strange evening. No matter how hard he pondered he couldn't work it out. For, how was Tommy to know that the theatre was about to close down – perhaps forever!

He got very little sleep that night as the place was full of people. No one seemed anxious to go home and the church bells were ringing before the last of them left. It felt as if he had just settled down when he heard a familiar voice calling him. It was J.P., an old friend, standing there with a strange box in his hand. He picked Tommy up and put him gently into the box. There was a sort of grille on the front which he closed, and this made Tommy very nervous indeed. He felt trapped, but J.P. put a finger through the bars and tickled him under the chin.

'Don't worry,' he soothed, 'you'll be home soon.'

That worried Tommy even more. He was at home, but this man he had always regarded as a friend was carrying him out of it. Out the stage door, into the sunlight and down the laneway into a street full of people. Tommy had never been so far away before and he peered out in fear and puzzlement. He saw to his horror that he was being put into one of those monsters that he sometimes saw through the theatre windows at night.

Noisy monsters with bright lights shining from their eyes. Then he realised it was moving and he gave a howl of dismay. A finger was poked through the bars and he considered biting it to show his displeasure. He decided against this – he was in enough trouble.

After what seemed hours they stopped moving and he was carried indoors again. The box was opened and he peered out hoping that he had returned home. But this was a strange place with a number of strange faces looking down at him. They were friendly faces and several hands reached down to pat him. He decided to leave the box before that door was shut again, and he ventured out to investigate.

It was a small room and as he nosed all round it he came across a fire. He remembered that other fire with the white rug and he waited for someone to shout, 'Get that cat out of here,' but no one did. Instead, a big basket was produced and he was put down on a soft woolly blanket. He had never stretched out in front of a fire before and it was so delightful that he almost forgot about the way he had been kidnapped. He watched the flames flickering in the fire and the smoke disappearing through a dark hole. Maybe I could escape through that hole, he thought. He stretched forward to get a better look, and then smelt something burning – that was the end of his whiskers! No escape that way, he decided.

As if reading his thoughts someone opened the door and said, 'Come on, puss, have a look around.'

Tommy went from room to room, upstairs and downstairs. It was much smaller than his theatre, but warm and comfortable. Everyone seemed friendly and glad he was there and in one room he found his very own dish full of his favourite food.

But the biggest surprise was yet to come.

A big glass door was opened and outside in the sunlight was a long green carpet.

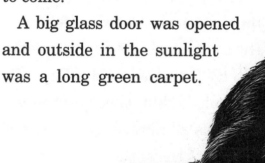

Tommy had never seen real grass before and as he trotted through it a flock of small birds flew away. Flying mice, thought Tommy, just like the one that landed on those lady musicians. He waited for them to land so that he could chase them again, but they remained twittering in a tree above him. The tree looked stronger than the one he had knocked down the day he met the cat man, so Tommy decided to climb it. He found he could get up if he dug his nails in, but as he reached the top the birds all flew away to another tree.

Then Tommy discovered that it was much easier to get up a tree than to get down it! He was sure those birds were giggling at his efforts, so he let out a wail of annoyance and finally someone came to his rescue. Then Tommy hid under the tree until the birds came down again and he dashed out and scattered them in all directions. He had a wonderful day chasing the 'flying mice' and as darkness fell he was called in. He felt really hungry after all the exercise and devoured a big dish of food. Then he stretched out in his basket before the fire and was joined by his new family. It was strange to look around and see all those feet. Strange, but very comforting.

Each day was a new adventure. He climbed trees, chased birds and explored other gardens. One day he went out and found water pouring from the sky. That was the day he discovered rain, which he did not like very much. Another morning he looked out and the grass was gone. Everything was white. That was the day he discovered snow,

which was great fun until you came
back into the house with muddy paws.

One day he pushed his way through a
hedge and a big black dog chased him.
He was afraid that Madame Fifi and her
pack had tracked him down. He peeped

back through the hedge and saw the dog burying a bone in the ground. So, they were hiding their food now to stop him getting it. He watched for some time but the others dogs and Madame Fifi did not appear. Tommy decided that this was a different dog with an unusual way of hiding his food.

Shortly after this Tommy looked into another garden and saw a man burying food, just like the black dog! The man made holes in the ground, put in little pieces of food and then covered them up carefully. When the man had gone away Tommy thought he would like to taste some of this food. It was no trouble to dig up the pieces from the soft earth, but they tasted awful. Some of them even made his eyes water. Suddenly, the man rushed out of his house, shouting and roaring. Tommy dashed home, followed closely by the man. He hid under a table. He could hear the man complaining bitterly about the cat stealing his onions. He was a big fat man. Surely he would not miss a few pieces of food. As a matter of fact it would do that man a lot of good to miss lots of food. But the man was getting a great deal of sympathy at the door and Tommy wondered what was going to happen to him. When the man had gone Tommy jumped up on the couch and did his turning around trick. That had always made people laugh. Unfortunately, nobody laughed this time as Tommy had forgotten that his paws were very dirty from digging in the garden. So, for the rest of the night, he kept out of the way and hoped for the best.

Chapter 6

Home Again

WHEN J.P. PICKED HIM UP the following morning Tommy thought he had been forgiven, and he purred with satisfaction. Then, to his dismay, he was put into that awful box and the grille was closed. He was carried outside to the monster with lights in its eyes. As he was driven away he wondered what fate awaited him. A finger was pushed into the box to tickle him under the chin, and J.P. said, 'Don't worry, you'll be home soon.'

That was exactly what he had been told the last time he was kidnapped!

They stopped moving and he was carried outside. This laneway looked familiar. They went through a newly painted door and there was Fred, the stage doorman, saying, 'Hello Tommy, welcome home.' The box was opened beside Tommy's Room, but he hardly recognised it. It looked brand new and his star looked like real gold. He hurried inside and was delighted to find his old carpet on the floor.

The old theatre was shining and beautiful, freshly painted and polished, and Tommy could not wait to see it all. On the way upstairs he met the small lady with glasses who gave him a hug. As if by magic the men with the cameras flashed their lights at them, but this time the lady was smiling and laughing. The theatre was filling up with people. He must go and see what had happened to his favourite seat in his favourite box. It was gleaming in red and gold – that seat looked wonderful. He was just about to jump up on it when a group of people came in. He waited for the usual cry, 'Get that cat out of here.' Instead, a tall, important-looking man, that everyone called 'The President', patted him on the head, saying, 'Sorry to disturb you, puss. Isn't the old place looking marvellous? I'm sure you are very glad to be home again.'

He was.

More RED FLAG books from The O'Brien Press

THE GREAT PIG ESCAPE
Linda Moller
Illustrated by Kieron Black

Runtling the pig finds out that the trip to market is one he must avoid at all costs. He warns his twelve pig-mates and together they escape. They find an abandoned farm, but then new owners arrive and the pigs fear that their escape has been in vain. But Nick and Polly Faraway have strange, alternative ideas about farming and a lifestyle that might work to the benefit of pigs and humans. Maybe there can be a happy ending after all!

Paperback €6.50/STG£4.99

WOLFGRAN
Finbar O'Connor
Illustrated by Martin Fagan

Granny has moved into the Happy-Ever-After Home for Retirement Characters from Fairy Tales. But the Big Bad Wolf is still on her trail! Disguised as a little old lady, the wolf is causing mayhem as he prowls the city streets, swallowing anybody who gets in his way. Hot on his heels are Chief Inspector Plonker, Sergeant Snoop and a very clever little Girl Guide in a red hood. But will they get to the wolf before he gets to Granny?

Paperback €6.50/STG£4.99

ALBERT AND THE MAGICIAN

Leon McAuley
Illustrated by Martin Fagan

When the headmaster announces that The Great Gazebo is coming to visit the school, Albert's big sister, Fionnuala, tells him awful tales about the powers of magicians, especially over seven-year-old boys. Poor Albert is terrified! When a funny-looking old man turns up at the school gate on an old banger of a bike, Albert kindly helps him carry his bags – then, horror of horrors, he discovers that this is the magician ... and now he has a *special interest in Albert!*

Paperback €6.95/STG£4.99

Send for our full-colour catalogue